TALK
FROM THE
GREEN

Written by **MICHAEL DUKES**

Illustrated by **ABIGAIL OSHIRO**

A Talk from the Green
Pinecone Press, LLC
Sandy Springs, GA

ISBN: 978-1-7368463-0-8

Publisher's Cataloging-in-Publication data

Names: Dukes, Michael Y., author. | Oshiro, Abigail, illustrator.
Title: A talk from the Green / by Michael Dukes ; illustrated by Abigail Oshiro.
Description: Sandy Springs, GA: Pinecone Press, LLC, 2021. | Summary: Corvette is the patriarch of a family of grey squirrels who have lived on the grounds of Royal Greendale (the Green) for generations. Each Spring, Corvette and his wife Gertie must impart upon that year's litter the wisdom of life on the Green.
Identifiers: ISBN: 978-1-7368463-1-5 (hardcover) | 978-1-7368463-0-8 (paperback)
Subjects: LCSH Squirrels--Juvenile fiction. | Golf--Juvenile fiction. | Humorous stories. | Squirrels--Fiction. | Golf--Fiction. | BISAC JUVENILE FICTION / Sports & Recreation / Golf | JUVENILE FICTION / Animals / Squirrels.
Classification: LCC PZ7.1.D8346 TAL 2021 | DDC [Fic]--dc23

JUVENILE FICTION / Sports & Recreation / Golf

Cover and Interior design by Victoria Wolf, wolfdesignandmarketing.com
Illustrations by Abigail Oshiro

QUANTITY PURCHASES: Schools, companies, professional groups, clubs, and other organizations may qualify for special terms when ordering quantities of this title. For information, email michael@pinecone-press.com.

PINECONE PRESS

This clever little story, which covers so much more than the creatures of the Green, is dedicated to my wonderful family, and everything that it will become.

Preface

IT'S FATHER'S DAY TODAY. For my family, that means it's time for the Talk.

I love to tell stories, always have, and so I'm guessing I'll digress here and there – I always do. But I've figured out that as each season comes and goes, if you really open your eyes and pay attention to the world around you, it's amazing how full and interesting life is.

Royal Greendale, or "the Green" as the Whacks call it, is one of the special places on earth – a self-contained ecosystem full of life. When I give the Talk, I try to include everything and everybody. Usually not ten minutes after I wrap it up, I find myself scurrying down the sunny side of the Big Pine, chasing the kids to tell them just one more nugget.

"Got it, Dad!"

"Gee thanks, Dad!"

"Hey Dad, can we please keep moving – nineteen branches down already, three to go before the trunk, and we want to play – you can tell us more at bedtime."

"Okay, okay, I get it – go have fun and be safe. We'll be watching from halfway up, you know the spot."

My name is Corvette T. Pinecone VII (that's the 7th), and like my dad, and his dad, and four or five more before them, I've got the special gene that lets me understand the world of the Whacks. I can hear the Whacks, and kind of understand them. The gene lets me into their world a little, which is always fun because they can be the dumbest creatures in all the Green – in fact, I'm convinced they *are* the dumbest creatures in all of the Green.

Royal Greendale – the Green – is the world we live in, and it's a golf course. One of the nicer ones around, the Whacks say, although they're always talking about other courses all over the world – which ones they've played, who's winning the tournament this week, and where it is. Plus, they talk about the green speed on the stimp, undulations, pin placement, break, grain, rough height, par, par, par, birdie, birdie, birdie, bogey, bogey, bogey, slice, draw, cut, punch, fade, hook, and drive, blah blah blah blah blah. They never stop talking about that game they play ...

Anyway, the Green is our world. Gertie and I have twelve little eyes this year looking up at us on the Platform, sixty feet straight up the trunk of the Big Pine. From there, the view is incredible. We look out toward the morning sun and can see almost the whole place. Every time I take a moment to soak in that view, it warms my heart – I'll never get tired of it.

Three girls and three boys – the most we've ever had in the nest – and all ready to scamper out into the world. Thus, the need for the Talk. It's the most important thing I do each year. It's hard to tell if it works or even how to measure success, but I feel pretty good about it when I sit up on my furry little hind legs on the Platform, look out over the Green, and spot the nests of sixteen of our kids high in their own trees. They all had the Talk seasons back, so it must've been all right.

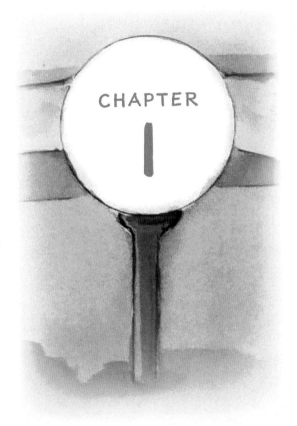

CHAPTER

1

THE GREEN

"OKAY KIDS, COME ALONG NOW – out to the platform – it's time for a little talk."

At that, three cute feisty little he-squirrels bounded through the sleep nest, pushing and tugging, trying to make their way through the tiny little door which only a few short weeks ago seemed so huge to them. It's amazing how fast they grow. At this point, the eight of us can hardly fit in the sleep nest. Out popped the other three – the little ladies of the nest – with the pretty little eyelashes they'll grow into.

When the nest becomes tight like it is, the weather has finally warmed up, and the leaves have filled out in all the trees, it's once again time for the little ones to move on. They won't go far, and they'll always be in sight. They'll be on their own, but we'll still assemble right here at this spot to hear the stories and adventures of the day.

"Okay everybody, as you probably know by now, nature is kind of pulling you away from the nest. You're feeling the excitement of getting out on your own and exploring our world your own way. But before we give you the green light (that's a Whack term – no idea where it came from), your mother and I want to give you the rundown of our world."

I continued, "We live in a special world. If you look out toward the rising sun, you see big buildings, cars, concrete, and roofs as far as the eye can see. If you scan across in all directions, you see nothing but the same. But if you tighten up your view, you'll see that our world, where we live, is nothing but forest, meadows, lakes, and rolling hills. That's because we live on Royal Greendale, or "the Green," as we all call it. The Green is what the Whacks call a golf course, and the beauty of the Green is that the Whacks take care of it and consider it a retreat from the hustle and bustle of the crazy Whack world."

"Um, Daddy," cute little She-squirrel #2 interrupted.

"Yes dear?"

"Umm, have you ever been away from the Green and in the Whack world?"

"Yes, I have dear, and that's a story for another time. As you've probably noticed," I kept going, "we squirrels aren't the only creatures living here, and I'm going to give you the rundown of who else is out there. Okay so far?"

"Daddy?" asked She-squirrel #2.

"Yes dear?"

"I already know a few other creatures."

"Is that right? Tell me about that, little girl."

"Well, I'm already friends with a bluebird chick," she said as her little eyelashes batted up and down shyly.

"That's great. The more friends you can make in the Green, the better," I said.

"Let's get started. Here's the rundown on the Green. The

Green is basically a string of eighteen or nineteen meadows, all linked together from start to finish, but in a winding, twisting kind of way. The meadows are separated by forest or brush, but from one, you can see another one or two. From up here, if you pay attention closely, you'll see them all, and they form a big, big circle. On the edge of the whole Green, there is a Whack-made fence of metal and wire of different sizes."

I asked, "Can you see that metal and wire? That's a Whack fence. If you see this fence, you'll know you are way too close to the edge of Whack world. Turn around right away and head back to the middle of the Green. If you don't remember anything else I say today, remember that. Outside of the Whack fence is a totally different world. Soon you'll hear of some of the many dangers that lurk within the Green, but if you step outside of the fence, those dangers to you multiply by ten. Never, ever, ever cross through the fence. Got it, everybody?"

Twelve little eyes looked up at me as wide as I'd ever seen them. We hate to have to talk about dangers, but the reality is that they exist, and there are many of them, so it's better to be aware. That's part of our job as parents.

"The creatures living in the Green with us are everywhere, and I'm about to get into who they are and how they live, but you need to understand a few more things about the Green. Creatures who live here can generally be considered Front-siders or Back-siders, part-timers or full-timers, visitors, friends, or threats."

"So, what makes a Front-sider a Front-sider like us, Daddy?" asked He-squirrel #3.

"Great question, buddy. Front-side and Back-side are Whack terms that describe the two main sections of the Green. If you look out toward the sunrise spot, past the four or five closest meadows, and just to the right of the Grandpa Oak, you'll see the little Whack road that runs across the Green. That road divides the Green between its Front-side and its Back-side. You'll hear the Whacks talking about it all the time, so we kind of use the term too. We're considered Front-siders."

Off in the distance, the distinct sound that starts this time of day was obvious: . Wait one minute, then again *Whack.*

Two more times, then quiet again. "Anybody know that sound yet?"

I heard six little giggles. "Of course we do, Daddy. It's the first group of Whacks of the day," said She-squirrel #1.

So the talk began.

CHAPTER
2

TIME

"BEFORE WE TALK ABOUT ALL THE CREATURES in the Green, let's talk about the basics of time. Every single morning, the sun rises from the east, moves across the sky getting stronger as it gets right above us, and then it slowly starts losing its energy and strength as it sinks off to the west until finally it's gone."

I continued, "As soon as the sun leaves for the day, the moon peeks its head out, and it rises and sets just like the sun does, although it is way dimmer and weaker than the sun. In fact, it never really lights things up very well, and it also never makes things any warmer. The moon has this strange cycle where it starts out almost not being there at all – hardly any light. Then it gets bigger and brighter each day, starting out like a thin smile and filling out each day until it shows up as a full circle, as bright as it can get. The Whacks call this the full moon. Then it gets dimmer and dimmer until it's totally out of sight, and the cycle starts over again.

"Okay, so we have the sun and the moon – everybody got it so far? Next up are the seasons," I continued. "Another strange cycle that always happens like clockwork. Even though the sun feels warm right now, its strength changes throughout the year. Soon, the sun will lose its strength, and when it does, all the bright green leaves on all the trees will turn red, or yellow, or brown, and fall to the ground. The Whacks call this season the fall – when all the leaves fall down.

"After fall, the sun gets even weaker and only stays out half of the day, and it never really warms anything up. This season is called the winter. In the winter, we'll spend a lot of time in our cozy nests." I smiled at the babies.

"Winter comes and winter goes, and soon, the sun starts getting its strength back. And as it does, little green buds start popping out of the tree branches. Also, little green sprouts start popping up out of the ground and turn into flowers, and the whole Green lights up in pretty colorful flowers. This season is called spring."

I looked around at my little ones, and they were listening. I kept going. "And finally, after spring, the sun gets its brightest and hottest. All the trees are full of bright green leaves, and all the Green's meadows are green. There is green everywhere!" I added with excitement.

"The final season is called summer – and we're in it right now. And there you have it: the basics of time here in the Green ..."

"Um, Daddy, as complicated as it all sounds, it seems pretty simple too. Like, at any point in time, you should know where you are in the cycle, and you can also trust that the cycle will happen again – just like it has for you and Mom and all the other Corvette T. Pinecones," said little He-squirrel #1, ever the logical thinker.

"Sounds like you've learned a little bit today, buddy, which means I've done my job," I said with a wink toward Gertie.

CHAPTER

3

WE'RE NOT ALONE

"NOW LET'S GET TO THE FUN PART – the creatures of the Green," I continued.

"First up – our closest cousins, the chipmunks. They are Front- and Back-siders, full-timers, great friends, but total pigs when it comes to eating and saving acorns and nuts for the winter. They can fit six acorns in their cheeks at once. I've seen it with my own eyes!"

My kids nodded and giggled. "Next up – bunny rabbits. They are also Front- and Back-siders, full-timers, and great friends. Every time you turn around, all the she-bunnies have a nest full of babies – all year long, not just in the spring like us."

I said, "Now let's talk about deer. They are also Front-
and Back-siders, full-timers, and great friends, but there's
a couple of weird things to remember. First, the male deer –
or Bucks, as they're called – have big horns that grow until
the winter, then fall off and start growing again. Second,
the male deer are as nice as can be all year except for their
grumpy moon, when they act like they have never seen you
before, are no longer your friends, and run around chasing
she-deer like crazy all hours of the day."

Six little faces looked up at me, and I said, "Now we'll talk about the first kind of Whack, the best kind of all: the Creature-Whack. They act more like us than most Whacks. While you're watching his group on the meadow, you'll notice he's watching you or other creatures and enjoying seeing what we do. You can tell he has a kind heart and an appreciation for nature. This kind of Whack loves to drop sunflower seeds from his bag for you as you watch his partners whack away."

Since there were no questions, I continued. "Mourning doves are the first birds we'll talk about. They are so import- ant because every morning, they fly out and circle the entire Green and come back to report if things look okay. Since birds can fly, they aren't really considered Front-siders or Back-siders.

"Possums are interesting. You'll not see them very often. They like to sleep in their dens almost all day and only come out at night to look for food and scamper around. A fun thing to see is a mother possum with a litter of eight to ten babies. They cling and crawl around on her as she walks.

"And now back to birds – Cardinals and Guardinals, the red cardinals, are all over the Green and are some of our closest friends. They are hard workers, always building nests, finding berries to eat, digging for worms, and feeding their chicks.

"Guardinals are totally different. They spend their time flying around certain Whacks, trying to get their attention. Several seasons back, I had a conversation with one of these guys, and it finally all made sense. Guardinals are sent here from God with a special mission. Their role is to show Whacks that things they don't understand are going to be okay. You see, Whacks don't always understand the cycle of life, so they're often trying to change things or make things their own. They are big worriers too – about anything you could imagine. It's not their fault; it's just their instinct.

"So, the Guardinals will find a sad or worried Whack, fly somewhere close, and get their attention by fluffing up and sitting on a branch for a little bit longer than normal until the Whack realizes something different is going on. Suddenly, the Whack feels comforted and relaxes because of the reminder that God loves them and that everything's gonna be okay."

CHAPTER
4

THE SHAKE

I LOOKED OVER AT GERTIE and across the platform at the kids who still looked pretty engaged. He-squirrels #2 and #3 were kicking each other, and He #1 was laughing at his brothers. Of course, the she-squirrels were paying close attention as they always did.

In the distance, I heard, *shake, shake, shake* – and then *shake, shake, shake* – and then *shake, shake, shake* again. The shakes got closer and closer to us and then moved farther away.

"You kids know what that is?" I asked. "I'm feeling a little rumbly in my tummy, so I think it's a good time to take a quick family excursion," I added.

"You ever notice that late in the afternoon, Mom and I pop into the nest with pretty yellow corn kernels for you?"

"Oh yes, Daddy! Is it time? Might be one of my favorite times of the day. We'll be right here waiting," said little She #3 ... who always looked forward to our heads popping into the nest with a little treat.

"This is going to be a family adventure. Every afternoon, our Border-Whack, who lives in the Whack nest right down there, brings out corn and tosses it across the fence to feed the deer. When you hear the *shake, shake, shake*, you know it's time for a little snack."

"But Daddy, should we be eating it?" asked She #2, with the cute little concerned face she always made. "Isn't the corn for the deer?"

"Wait, you'll see. There is more corn on the ground than any deer could ever enjoy in one sitting. We better hurry, though, every other creature in the Green knows that sound too."

"We?" She #1 cried out. "Daddy, 'we' wouldn't mean 'us,' would it?"

The cautious little angel always cracked me up. "Yep, you got it! Let's go everybody, follow me!" I called. "Come on – we're burning daylight!"

I hopped across the platform, pounded through the nest like a wild animal, bounced through the other side and across the branch toward the trunk. At the main trunk, I stopped in the notch and turned around to watch. The he-squirrels bounced out first, laughing and jumping for position, scampering along the branch coming right at me.

"Whoa! Slow down you goofballs, you're gonna knock me outta the tree," I screamed.

Slowly the she-squirrels made it through the nest and hopped our way. She #3 was having a little trouble getting over the nest entrance but made it just fine.

We all paused at the notch, a teaching moment ...

"So, kids, always remember this. You see where we are headed, and that there are two ways to get there?"

We all looked sixty feet down and across the pine-straw-covered ground below us to where the Border Whack had thrown a bucketful of corn over his fence onto the edge of the Green.

"We could race straight down the Big Pine, then hop across the ground to get there, or we could shoot straight across this branch, hop over to that leaf-covered oak branch, and make our way down the oak straight to where the corn is.

"Any time you have the choice, no matter where you're going," I said seriously, "it's always best to take the high route and avoid the ground as much as possible. There is safety high in a tree – and danger on the ground – just keep this in mind and always be smart."

We hopped out and nearly to the end of the long, skinny pine branch and then onto the leafy oak branch, making our way to the massive trunk. Then we hesitated, scouted the area, and circled the huge oak trunk all the way down to the ground. Instinct is an amazing thing, I thought, as I looked up and watched my new season family scurry down the oak. You'd think they'd done it a thousand times. Gertie and I sat back on the top of the fence post and watched the little ones fill up on corn kernels.

Gertie heard it first – her furry tail went straight up into the air and she barked loudly – it sent chills down my spine. Again, instinct is an amazing thing. All six of the kids heard Mom's bark, saw her tail, and were twenty feet up the oak before I could finish turning my head. Not too dangerous; it was just a Whack looking for his ball close to the border fence.

Any time a ball comes over here, you know it's a Hack-Whack. It's a funny kind of Whack. They get told time and time again to simply keep their head still, don't sway, do a full shoulder turn, keep the clubhead down, not across, swing inside out, and follow through. What do they do every time? The exact opposite, which is why he was walking through the woods close to the fence looking for his ball. That's one thing I'll never understand about Whacks. The golf swing is so simple, so fluid, so natural, but when Whacks over-think it, they end up hunting for their balls in the woods and mumbling. But, they never stop coming back. The Green must be really appealing to them.

"Great job reacting to Mom's bark everybody. Just sit tight here for a few minutes, and he'll move on. But remember, you can't always count on Mom being here, so you guys need to pay attention and be on the lookout for danger at all times. I want to see some of you start being the ones making the bark and fluffing your tails."

"Got it, Dad!" said the ever-brave He #3. "I think he's gone now."

"Yes, it's all clear. Let's have a couple more pieces of corn, then head back up to the platform," I said.

The whole crew made it up and around the towering oak's trunk, across the longest branch on the setting sun side, hopped onto the pine branch, across to the trunk of Big Pine, up a few more branches, through the nest, and plopped onto the platform. I was pretty impressed and satisfied with our excursion. Once everyone settled in and got comfortable, I got back to the Talk.

CHAPTER

5

DANGER

"SO, KIDS, NOW WE NEED TO TALK about the danger creatures in the Green. Your instinct will tell you right away if one is in the area, but let's go through the list just to make sure. These creatures are bad news and wouldn't hesitate for two seconds to attack and eat you. That's just a fact of life. The reality is, they're creatures just like us. The problem is that they need to eat, and their instinct tells them that squirrel meat is tasty – just like we think acorns are tasty.

"It's part of everyone's daily jobs to be alert for these guys and immediately warn all other creatures if we see one. Here's a thought to ponder, and it's based on a Whack saying:

In Africa (which is a faraway land, but a lot like the Green, as best as I can figure), when the sun rises, the gazelle awakens and knows that today it must run faster than the lion, or it will be eaten. On that same morning, the lion awakens and knows that today it will have to run faster than the gazelle, or it will go to bed hungry. Thus, the common theme in Africa – when the sun comes up, you better be running.

Immediately, He #1 picked up on the idea, and one by one, the rest of the crew did as well. Needless to say, there were some squirming little squirrels on the platform.

"Now listen, guys, there's nothing to be scared of, as long as you are always aware of your surroundings and always know your escape route. Eyes and ears peeled at all times – that's all," I told them, trying for a little reassurance.

"Now, back to the Talk and the dangers," I said.

"Coyotes generally den on the Back-side down in the deep dark hollow near the creek bottom," I began. "That is one place never to visit, no matter what. They are sneaky, fast, and love the taste of us squirrels, bunnies, birds, and anything else they can get their paws on. They wait for one of us to cross a meadow during daylight. That's why I have told you to never ever cross a meadow, the Whacks call them fairways, on the ground. There are ways to the other side up in the air. Most squirrels only make this mistake once – got it?"

By now, the she-squirrels were trembling, and a little tear came out of She #3's little puffy eye. Gertie rubbed her head and reminded us that this is part of the reason for the Talk – we need to know the dangers out there, and this was Numero Uno!

"Another danger creature is the hawk. Hawks don't really live in or out of the Green; they just soar through the sky like an airplane and are a threat from above. That's why it's so important to be aware of danger from all angles," I continued.

"Owls usually live in nests in rotten trees in the Green. Unlike the hawks, though, owls are nighttime creatures and are a danger to us early in the morning or right before dark," I said. "Surprisingly, they aren't crazy about us for food. They like mice and moles better."

"Now let's talk about snakes," I went on. "There are snakes of different shapes and sizes all over the Green. The small garden snakes are actually friendly. They spend most of their time slithering around the grass and bushes, looking for crickets, bugs, and the occasional berry. The most dangerous is the dreaded rat snake. He is long – maybe even as long as a tree branch, and mainly dark-colored with a white belly.

"Okay, enough of the scary stuff, let's talk about some of the funny creatures in the Green: the pond and water creatures.

"Turtles may be slow moving, but they have a great sense of humor. In fact, my closest friend in the whole world is Mr. Theodore T. Turtle. If you remember me mentioning being out of the Green, well, it was Ted and me who found ourselves away from the Green many seasons ago," I shuddered. "Thank goodness that story is behind us."

"Daddy, umm, are you ever gonna tell us why you were away from the Green?" asked She #1, with her concerned eyes blinking and her little nose crumpled up.

"Sweetie, Daddy may tell you that story one day, but not today," Gertie chimed in.

Thank goodness she did because I'm not crazy about telling that story. All worked out okay in the end, but boy, was it bad. Maybe one day ...

"One water creature is the grass carp, a huge, whale-looking fish you see swimming along the surface in the ponds right after the Green Whacks finish cleaning the meadows with their machines," I continued, even though I was getting tired. "The grass carp are fun to watch 'cause they're big and lazy. All they do is swim around, open their big mouths at the surface of the pond, and catch all the junk floating on the surface."

I paused. Five of the six sets of eyes looking up at me were getting heavy, and I knew it was time to stop.

"Okay, everybody, what do you say we slip over into the nest and settle in for the night? I'm getting sleepy myself."

It didn't take long for the babies to sit up, stretch, shake their little fluffy tails, and hop back into the nest. By the time I hopped into my corner of the nest, the rest of the crew was all curled up and comfy.

"Goodnight my children. We'll finish the Talk tomorrow."

Six soft little voices of our babies said, "Goodnight Mommy and Daddy," and the day was behind us once again. I must say there is a lot of peace for a Mom and Dad in knowing that everyone in the family is tucked in and sleeping safely. Gertie curled up next to me, put her head across my back, and whispered a quick, "Goodnight Corvette."

GREEN MACHINES AND CLOSE ENCOUNTER

JUST ABOUT THE TIME I WAS EXPECTING IT, I heard the first bird chirp and saw the first hint of light coming through the tattered entrance to the nest. All six babies had grown in the past week, and it was tight in the nest. I love waking up and seeing them curled up on top of each other; feet covering eyes, tails used like pillows, and He #2 stretched out lengthwise across the bodies of the others like he was on top of a big feather bed.

As the light strengthened and the birds of the Green began their morning songs, I hopped out onto the platform and stretched. My feeling about today was confirmed with a roar. Out across the meadow, up over the hill, and headed in our direction were the three huge green machines that show up every few days in a perfect line. These machines were driven by the Green-Whacks, and best as I can tell, their purpose is to cut the grass of the meadows low and tight and blow the clippings off the grass.

Most of the time, the green machines show up at different times during the day and are gone pretty quickly, but as I suspected, this was the special day – the day the Whacks call Saturday.

On Whack-Saturday, the green machines show up right at the crack of dawn and work fast. Following the green machines is a group of Green-Whacks who walk with rakes and blowers and tidy up the meadow to the point where it almost looks as tidy as the inside of our nest after Gertie's incessant cleaning.

The reason Whack-Saturdays are special is that, not long after the green machines are gone, we hear the distant *Whack, Whack, Whack, Whack* usually four times in a row. As soon as the first group of Whacks shows up on our meadow, it is nonstop Whacks until almost sunset. This is the ideal day for Whack observation!

"Okay kids, time to get moving – we're burning daylight!"

Gertie looked over at me with her typical smile. Rather than objecting and slowing me down, she gave me the nod and was up on her feet helping to get the kids moving.

"Daddy, what are you and Mommy gonna bring up for

breakfast this morning? I'm kind of hungry," said She #3.

"Sweetheart, I'm glad you asked!" I boasted, getting the full attention of the whole nest.

"Today is going to be something totally new. Instead of Mommy and me scampering off to find your breakfast, we're *all* getting up and going off together on another excursion!"

"Yes! Yes! Yes!" blurted the three he-squirrels with high-fives all around.

"Today is a Whack-Saturday, the best day of all to observe the Whacks and learn a little more about all the different shapes and colors they come in.

"We're gonna scamper across five pines, then three oaks, then two more pines, and then down to the ground. That'll get us to the end of our meadow to a spot the Whacks call the tee," I told them.

"It's the spot that every meadow has, where the Whacks all whack from the same spot. This time of year, the tee is surrounded by beautiful pink azaleas and tons of honey-suckle. Even better, there are always leftover acorns blown into the azaleas by the Green-Whacks."

At that, this year's family of Corvette T. Pinecone VII (that's the 7th) took off for a day of Whack-Saturday watching. What a perfect way to learn the Whack piece of the Talk in living color! Off they scurried, high in the canopy. Trunk turning to branch, branch getting skinnier, skinnier, skinnier – now flimsy – quick hop, now a skinny branch, but with leaves, then thicker, thicker, sturdier, then another trunk.

And so the cycle went until I gave the signal it was time to head straight down a trunk. Then, one by one, the rest of the family made their way down to the ground into a thick, bushy azalea garden. In person, the flowers were almost the size of a grown-up squirrel. The dew inside the petals tasted like lemonade to the little ones.

The azaleas formed a huge semicircle around a tightly mowed tee. It was great cover because the green leaves, pink flowers, and occasional honeysuckle vines were so thick, a squirrel could move along the ground in and among the plants without being seen – but could also get a great view of the tee without looking obvious.

"Okay, everybody gather around. I just heard a couple of Whacks the next meadow over, which means the first group will be here in a few minutes. Here's the plan: we're gonna spread out all along the azaleas and dig around and find acorns buried in the mulch – like we're not up to anything but breakfast. When the Whacks show up, you'll know it. Just find yourself a spot, sit back on your hind legs with an acorn in your hands, and watch how funny they are. Make sure to keep the rest of the family in a direct line of sight at all times – and boys, no giggling!" I added, laughing myself.

"When each group moves on down the meadow, we'll gather back over by the big oak tree we descended, and I'll give you the rundown of the group and what kind of Whacks you just observed. Everybody got it?"

The look of excitement on their little faces was hilarious. Of course, She #2 was concerned, She #3 was more excited about the acorns, and the boys were just excited about finding the closest safe spot. I could feel the anticipation in the air.

Two carts came flying in, nearly on two wheels, then slammed their brakes to an immediate stop. The Whacks were talking so loudly you'd think they had hearing problems. I took my normal position directly behind the tee so I could watch the Whack from behind and see the ball fly up and across the pond, toward the tightly mown green. I looked around and, as instructed, the six youngsters had fanned out around the semicircle of azalea bushes, right at the base of the tee. Their eyes were doubly large out of excitement, fear, and worry, so I gave them a nod to remember to look natural. They all followed the order and watched as Whack No. 1 stepped out of the cart and walked straight to the back of the tee. The Whack was so close to He #3 and She #1 that I had a moment of panic, but as the Whack kept on walking to the tee, I stopped worrying.

To the babies, the Whack looked huge – as big as a pine tree from the ground. He walked up to the middle of the tee, set his feet in the ground, and swung his whacker back and forth a few times. He turned to the carts and yelled, "Sorry to do this to you, boys, but this will be close!"

And in return, there were chuckles, and a Whack from the cart yelled, "Fat chance, Jack Wagon." Then the entire group burst out in more laughter.

With his feet set in place, the Whack pulled the whacker back as he turned his body all the way back. Then, "whoosh," and faster than any of the babies could follow, he swung the whacker, and a loud "Whack" came from the ground. In astonishment, my family watched the little white ball leave the tee and fly through the air toward the target across the pond. But something was wrong – the ball didn't stay straight and get closer to the target, the flag on the green. Nope, instead, the ball started to shoot way high and to the right, almost as if a gust of wind turned its direction, and it flew way into the treetops to the right of the pond, not too terribly far from my family's nest.

Out of the blue, the Whack screamed, "Son of a Biiiisssscccuuuit!"

And the Whacks in the carts started laughing hysterically. Then he yelled something about his mother, which the family couldn't understand either. I knew exactly who this was – a Hack-Whack. From the moment he began his swing, I saw it coming: way too steep, club way off plane, downswing starts way over the top, swings across the ball from outside in, and sure enough, the power fade ... no, not really ... this was a flat-out banana slice – the calling card of the Hack-Whack.

Then the remaining three Whacks stepped up and went through their own goofy routines. Practice swings, balls whacked in all directions, cursing, laughing, and complete astonishment when the final Whack skulled his shot, and it shot right at the far side of the pond, bounced off the surface of the water, and skipped up across the green to within three squirrel lengths of the flag. The Whacks came unglued – laughing and carrying on – and then they were gone. The carts left and headed down to the other side of the pond, where the Whacks stormed through the woods looking for their balls.

At that point, as instructed, the family convened at the base of the big oak near the back of the semicircle of the tee.

"So, what'd you think, guys?" I asked.

"This is so much fun, Daddy. Can we stay? Please, please?" pleaded He #2.

"Okay, one more group. Now kids, remember, when the next group comes around the corner, spread out again and look natural. Hop around and stay close to the ground, and way out of their way," I reminded them.

"Look like you're digging for acorns or licking droplets off the azalea leaves – anything that makes you look uninterested. Do this, and you'll likely steer clear of danger. Got it?"

"Got it, Daddy," they replied in unison.

They heard another electric cart screaming in from above, but this one was slower and steadier, and a strange high-pitched voice came from the driver's side of the cart. As the cart rounded the bend and came into view, the family saw what appeared to be a father and son Whack twosome, and then, another. The kids were mesmerized. They hadn't ever thought about Whacks having babies just like squirrels do. As the carts came to a stop and the two father-and-son Whacks stepped out, I gave the reminder nod to "Get busy with looking natural!"

The kids did exactly as they were told, but then something different happened. Instead of marching straight to the tee like the Hack-Whacks had just done, the first father-and-son Whack pair walked toward the azaleas, ever so slowly, right toward me and He #1. We were lined up directly behind the tee for the swing analysis. The father held his son's hand and inched closer and closer to me. I immediately recognized the Creature Whack and knew this was about to get good.

"Look right there, son, look at that beautiful father squirrel, and look around. It looks like he has his young family out on an adventure this morning," the Father Whack said quietly. "Do me a favor – run back to the cart and get that bag of sunflower seeds. Hurry now!"

The young Creature Whack scurried off to the cart and came right back with a small bag in his hands.

"Son, slowly and gently toss a few seeds over in front of that big squirrel, then step back to me," said the Father Whack.

Sure enough, when there was plenty of distance, I nodded for He #1 to step up with me slowly, and we shared the small pile of sunflower seeds while the Creature Whacks watched joyfully.

"Son, there is more joy in the Green than whacking a white ball around. You just have to pay attention and observe the beauty," said the Father Creature Whack.

The boy smiled from ear to ear, and for a quick moment, my eyes locked with those of the Creature Whack, and He #1's eyes locked with those of the boy, and the bond was permanent.

The father and son teams whacked their balls and moved on, and I knew it was time to get back up to the nest. They could watch the rest of crazy Saturday from the safety above.

"Okay kids, that's it for today. Last one to the nest is a rotten egg!" I said, and they were off.

"I hope you learned a few lessons today. First, most Whacks pay you no attention, especially if you look natural and just mill around at a safe distance. Second, Whacks have this uncanny limitation in that they simply are too stupid to swing their whackers the way they are taught. Time and time again, even though they know to keep their swing on plane, to get a full shoulder turn, to swing through the ball from inside out, to swing smoothly, and follow through finishing facing their target – they simply cannot do it. They prefer to slice, hook, chunk, skull, and block their shots. This is one of those truths we'll never understand. And third, there are some genuinely awesome Whacks out there: kind, gentle, friendly, and respectful," I told them in awe. "These are the Whacks you'd like to get to know in your own way."

Then our little squirrels settled down into the sleeping nest for their evening prayers and bedtime story from their mom and me. As always, twelve little eyes grew heavy and closed not far into the story, which was by design. Watching children falling asleep with little smiles on their faces was yet another treat that Gertie and I could never get enough of.

CHAPTER
7

THE VISITORS

AFTER A GREAT RESTFUL SLEEP IN THE NEST, we heard the first chirps of the day sixty feet below. With a quick peek through the door to the platform, I could see the morning sky just starting to light up. Before long, the whole crew would be up and moving, so as always, I hopped out onto the platform to soak in the beauty of first light in the Green and ponder the day's activities. In reflecting on the Talk so far, I felt like I had covered most of what was needed, so today, I would cover the last piece I liked to call the visitors.

All the creatures in the Green I had talked about so far were permanent residents. I knew the migratory creatures who come and go through the Green at different times of the seasons would nicely round out the creature experience in the Green.

"Okay kids, hop on out onto the platform. The day is here, and it's time to get rolling!"

The six little siblings stretched, yawned, and pushed each other back and forth, making their way to the platform door. Out popped She #3, which made plenty of room for the rest, and within minutes, the platform was full of morning energy. The view across the Green at this time of day really was special. The damp morning smell of azaleas and honeysuckle filled the air. It all made me think:

What an incredible start to the day. What can I do today to make it even better than yesterday?

That's how I think, and it can be everything from annoying to infectious, depending on the day.

"Well good morning everyone," I said.

"Good morning, Daddy," the six youngsters responded in unison.

"Today we're going to talk about the creatures of the Green who we call visitors. So far, we have talked about everybody who will spend their whole lives here in the Green – like us. But there is a whole group of creatures out there that the Whacks call migratory."

"Daddy, is being a migratory a bad thing? Should we be scared?" whimpered little cautious She #2.

"No honey, not at all. Nature is surprising and constantly changing. It's another one of those things that we'll never fully understand. The visitors – the migratory creatures – have this inner pull in them that they can't do anything about. Just like we love the comfort of home and a permanent nest, they get this antsy feeling inside of them every time they sense the seasons changing. It makes them need to take off and find better weather.

"Most of the visitors are birds, but obviously not all birds are visitors. I've spoken to many of our visitor friends, and they tell me that it doesn't feel unusual to them at all. They just see it as having a summer home and a winter home, and in between is the long journey they take to get from one to another."

"Umm Daddy," asked little He #2, "how far of a journey do they take to get from one home to another?"

"Well, little buddy, I don't know for sure, but I know it's a long, long way. Mr. Mallard told me once that it takes him and his family three full moon cycles to get from his summer home to his winter home. He flies over hundreds and hundreds of Whack worlds and golf courses and forests twice every year. To sit back and listen to stories from his journeys is one of my favorite things to do every fall." I smiled as I thought about it.

"So, now let me tell you about some more of the visitors, and when we'll get to meet them. Mallards are ducks, and they can fly so fast and far, it is amazing. The Green is somewhere around the midpoint of their journey from their winter home way south near sunny beaches, and their summer home way north, where in the winter it is frozen solid nonstop. You can't miss them because the he-mallards have this big green shiny head, and the she-mallards are totally brown."

As I looked across the platform, I could see a couple of the babies giggling at the thought of a green-headed animal. A couple were completely astonished at the thought of the journey, and, of course, little She #3 was mainly thinking about breakfast.

"When will we see the green-headed mallards, Daddy?" asked curious and concerned little She #2, her lashes batting up and down as always.

"Sweetheart, they'll start showing up in early fall, which won't be long."

Then I said, "The next visitor we'll get to see is the hummingbird. The hummingbird is one of the most amazing creatures you'll ever see. Mainly because they are so tiny – no bigger than two acorns stacked on top of each other.

"They fly so fast that you really can't even see them when they're flying. The only time you can see them and talk to them is when they finally sit still on a branch."

"That sounds sooo cool, Daddy. When do we get to see these hummingbirds? I can't wait!" exclaimed little He #2.

"They'll start showing up pretty soon and will stay around for a couple of moon cycles. We'll hear them before we see them. When they fly, they make this loud buzzing sound that's hard to describe, but you'll know it when you hear it. It almost sounds like a giant bumblebee," I explained.

"Oh, and one more thing about hummingbirds," I continued, looking over at Gertie and noticing a little tear in her big brown eye.

"When I was away from the Green that one time, and very far away, I worried to death about how I would ever get back. I met a hummingbird named Ruby. It was Ruby who figured out that she would be stopping off at the Green soon, like she did twice a year on her journeys. And it was Ruby who took the news to your mother that late spring day that Ted the turtle and I were safe and slowly making our way back home."

"Daddy, Daddy, you have to tell us what that journey was all about!" demanded little She #2.

"Kids, that's a story for another day, but trust me, I'll tell you the whole story when the time is right. Just know that it sure was nice to get back home. Was it ever!

"The last visitors we'll talk about are the geese who come from a Whack world called Canada, which is a long way from here – way in the frozen north. The geese fly through the Green mainly in the early spring, and when they get here, we'll see them crash-land right in the middle of the pond over there, making a huge splash and honking loudly – almost like a crazy Whack car.

"The geese also build their nests on the ground near the ponds, and before you know it, there are huge families of geese walking around and honking all through the Green. I know you'll make great friends with their little fuzzy geese babies."

I looked across the platform and noticed something that was really out of character. Two of the girls were whispering and giggling to themselves instead of paying strict attention. "Well, well, young ladies," I said in a history teacher kind of way. "Do you have something you want to share with us all?"

She #3 pushed She #2 right in front of her, and She #2 had no choice but to ask, "Daddy, can you tell us about some of the other kinds of Whacks? I mean, She #3 and I saw one today that we can't stop laughing about. This crazy Whack got so mad after he hit his ball, he threw his whacker into the middle of the lake!" screamed She #2, and immediately the whole platform erupted with little squirrel giggles.

"Ah yes, my dear," I started. "What you witnessed today was a Hot-Head Whack. They normally have a terrible swing, dress like they are professionals, are always running their mouths to their buddies, and when they hit a bad shot, you better duck for cover!

"And the list goes on and on. You have Fast Whacks, Slow Whacks, Walker Whacks, Sandbagger Whacks, Gambler Whacks, Rough Whacks, Duff Whacks, Radar Whacks, Two Finger Putt Whacks, Beer Whacks, Smoke Whacks ..." At this point, Gertie interrupted. "Corvette – don't you think that's enough? I think they get the point," she said with a wink.

CHAPTER

8

NEST
TIME

I KNEW THE TALK WAS about wrapped up for now. There would always be more creatures who didn't make the cut for the Talk, but that was okay. I felt as if the kids had heard enough, and the rest would be up to them – with just a little guidance from Gertie and me – which never really ended.

"Okay crew, who's ready to head down to the ground and get some food?"

"Me, Daddy, Me, Daddy!" yelled little She #3 – no surprise there. And at that, we all took off as a family. We leapt off the platform, ran through the tight little entrance to the sleeping nest and out the other end, across the main branch sixty feet high in the Big Pine, and made our way down, and down, and down until we reached the pine-straw-covered ground.

As the kids scurried off in their own directions, Gertie and I could tell the time for them to be on their own was coming soon. Little He #2 and She #1 scurried off to the edge of the meadow to watch some silly Whacks who were trying to fish a ball out of the pond. He #1 and He #3 took off along a hedge to attack a honeysuckle vine that was full of flowers. And little She #2 and She #3 were moseying around, digging up acorns.

Now that the Talk was over, I knew that, before long, the family would be focusing on scoping out good nest spots close by, nest building, and acorn storage. As the seasons change, so do priorities. It was also about time for the annual naming ceremony for the family. Now that a whole spring had come and gone, we would give each of the little ones their official Green names.

I reached over and grabbed Gertie's hand and pulled her close. We shared a smile and could read each other's minds. *There is such peace, beauty, and joy in the Green ... the place we call home.*

THE END

About the Author

MICHAEL DUKES has spent more than 30 years in the corporate world as a CPA, consultant, investigator advisor, and mentor. Having lived most of his life on or around golf courses, and having played the game since his youth, his appreciation extends far beyond the game itself.

Now empty nesters, Dukes and his wife Mimi have raised three children and recently welcomed their first grandchild. Together they enjoy reflecting on how the parenting experience goes by in a flash- never really giving you enough time to fully impart your instinctive parental wisdom.

About the Illustrator

ABIGAIL HARUMI OSHIRO loves illustrating children's books especially when she is working in ink and watercolor.

Abigail grew up in California and graduated with a degree in fine arts with a specialization in illustration from California State University Long Beach. She currently lives in Atlanta where she works as a graphic designer and freelance illustrator.

You can see more of her art at, www.abbyoshiro.com and on Instagram: @abbyoshiro.art.

Made in the USA
Columbia, SC
10 May 2021